THE SUNSHINE TREE
and Other Tales
from Around the World

Retold by
Wendy Heller

Illustrated by
Brian O'Neill

GEORGE RONALD
OXFORD

GEORGE RONALD, Publisher
46 High Street, Kidlington, Oxford OX5 2DN, England

First Edition

ISBN 0-85398-153-1 Hardcover
ISBN 0-85398-154-X Softcover

A *Parents' and Teachers' Guide* to this book is available from the Publisher. (ISBN 0-85398-157-4)

Grateful acknowledgment is made to Blackie & Son Ltd for permission to adapt a story from *Tales from the Moors and Mountains* by Donald A. Mackenzie. The author wishes to express special thanks to Alfonso Escobedo for collecting and sending a version of "Many Ears of Corn."

The Publisher wishes to thank Norma O'Neill for her assistance in the design of this book

Printed in England by Billing & Sons Ltd., Worcester

CONTENTS

CONTENTS

Preface

The stories in *The Sunshine Tree* are based on folktales of many cultures. Some of the tales have grown out of stories that are hundreds and even thousands of years old. They have continued to be told and retold because they are still worth listening to.

Before writing came into common use, stories were kept alive by being passed on from one generation to the next by word of mouth. Part of the vitality of folktales was, and still is, in the story-telling event itself. No written version of a folktale can convey the magic combination of tale-teller and audience, just as reading a play cannot be compared to attending one. But then, the purpose of *The Sunshine Tree* is not to present a collection of folktales as they are told in the oral tradition. Its purpose is more like that of the fabulists, or fable-writers, of old. They drew freely on folktales about animals in order to write their own bird and beast stories. But under the feathers and fur, their fables were really about people.

Ever since writing was invented, writers have set down their own versions of folktales. Like other storytellers, writers have adapted the stories they chose to tell, keeping some elements, dropping others, and sometimes adding a few of their own.

In the oral tradition, folktales exist in many different versions. They have travelled around the world too, for people everywhere love to tell stories and are always eager to hear new ones. As the stories move from one culture to another, they become changed to fit the ways and customs of their new home. And as people themselves change, folktales change along with them, in order to fit the needs and beliefs of the people who tell them. The timeless and universal qualities remain, while outdated elements drop out.

Many old ideas no longer fit the way we think about our world and our fellow human beings, especially prejudices which held one group of people to be better than another, and which kept some groups of people from enjoying the equality that is their natural right. In retelling these stories for today, it has often been necessary to change them so that they do not reflect such prejudices.

Thus, the tales have been freely adapted, using a well-loved form from the heritage of the past to speak to some of the problems and challenges of the present. As each story-teller recreates a tale with each new telling, so each generation re-creates its own treasury of stories, to fit its own needs, for its own enjoyment, and as its own precious legacy to the future.

To Dan Jordan

Neighbours

Denmark

Once upon a time, a man and his wife received as their wedding gift a small farm in the middle of a wild heath, far from the village. Near the farm there was a low hill on top of which stood an old, tumbled-down ruin of stone. Happily, the couple went to live in their new home, but they soon found they were left all to themselves there. None of the villagers ever called on them for they were afraid to go near the hill, believing that fearsome hill-folk lived inside it. Although none of them had ever seen or talked to one of these hill-people, they were certain that they must be wicked and terrible, or at least very unpleasant.

But the couple paid no mind to such talk, and they enjoyed the peace and quiet of their home. One evening, as they sat by the fire, there came a knock at the door. The door opened and in strode a little man no more than knee-high, with a long beard, a red cap on his head, and wearing a leather apron.

At once they realized that the visitor must be one of the hill-people, but he did not look wicked or terrible, or even unpleasant. Although he looked different from themselves, he seemed friendly enough, and they invited him to sit down with them beside the fire.

'Good evening,' said the visitor. 'We people of the hill can see that you have come here to live, and our king has sent me to tell you that we wish you no harm. If you will leave us in peace and not torment us, we shall do the same for you.'

'You need fear nothing from us,' answered the man. 'We don't intend to harm you or your people. There is plenty of room for us all here. I don't know any reason why we shouldn't live as neighbours in peace and friendship.'

'Yes, won't you join us for supper?' said the woman.

'Thank you, no,' said the little man, bowing low, 'for my king will be anxious to hear this good news, and I must not keep him waiting. Goodnight!' And with that, he left just as suddenly as he had come.

Time passed and the couple lived in peace with the hill-folk. At first, the shy little people ran away when their neighbours approached, but after a while the hill-folk saw that the man and his wife truly meant them no harm, so they openly went about their business. And whenever the man and woman met their neighbours on the path, they always smiled and greeted them with a friendly word. The couple were delighted when, after the birth of their daughter

Ingrid, at their door they found a small basket filled with tiny cakes, a gift from the hill-people.

One day, not long afterwards, the woman became very ill, and her husband feared she might die. Straight away, he went to the village to seek help. He went to one person after another, but no one knew how to treat her illness. At last the villagers sent him to an old woman who had knowledge of herbs and curing. But she refused to go to see the sick woman because the house lay in the wild heath where the hill-folk dwelt. In spite of his pleading, she would not go beyond the edge of the village. The man went home very sad.

Night after night he watched over his wife helplessly, as she lay suffering. One evening, as he sat by her side, he fell asleep. Suddenly he woke up with a start, surprised to see that the room was full of hill-folk. One was sweeping the room, another was mending clothes, a third was rocking the baby, and a fourth was making a herbal tea, which she gave to the sick woman. But when the hill-people saw that the man was awake, they all ran out of the house. The very next day, the woman began to feel much better, and soon she was well enough to rise from her bed and return to her work.

The years passed, and Ingrid grew older. And the people of the hill continued to do kindly deeds for the family. In gratitude, Ingrid and her mother often took their neighbours dishes of porridge and round loaves of freshly baked bread.

One day, in the spring, Ingrid and her parents were surprised to find that all the stones in their field had been gathered up and piled to one side. And in the fall, when harvest time came, they found all the grain harvested and threshed, so that they did not have to do all the work themselves.

Many evenings they sat by their fire and talked about the many ways the hill-folk had helped them and what they might do to be of service to them in turn. And when they said their prayers at night, they thanked God for giving them the people of the hill as neighbours.

Late one evening, there was a knock at the door. It was the hill-man who had first visited them long ago. But this time, instead of his usual dress, he wore travelling clothes. Instead of his tools, he carried a walking stick. His face was very sad. 'My king requests you and your family to come to our dwelling this night,' he said. But he would tell no more.

That night Ingrid and her parents went to the cave where the hill-folk lived. They entered the little door in the side of the hill and went inside. They found themselves in a hall decorated with many-coloured wild flowers and bunches of fragrant herbs. A long, low table filled the room.

The king bade them sit in the seats of honour, and

the hill-people sat down as well. After they had eaten their meal, the king spoke. 'I have asked you to come here this night to tell you how grateful my people and I are for your friendship all these years. Alas, the time has come for us to leave this place and follow those of our people who crossed the water to Norway long ago. We must say farewell to you.'

One by one, the little people approached their neighbours to say good-bye. When they came to Ingrid, each of them took up a small stone from the ground and put it into her hands. Then they left their cave home and started off across the wild countryside, with their king leading them.

From the top of the hill, Ingrid and her parents watched them and did not turn to go home until the last of the hill-folk had disappeared into the night. Then, sadly, they went back to their house.

The next morning, Ingrid thought to look at the stones that the hill-folk had given her. But the stones which had seemed dull and plain in the dark night were plain no longer. They glittered and shone in the morning sun. Some were brown, some violet, others black, green, and blue. The hill-folk had given the stones the colour of their own eyes so that Ingrid would always remember them. Some say all precious stones have their lovely colours and shine so brightly only because the hill-folk once gave them the colour of their eyes, as a gift to their kindly neighbours.

The Fox's Tale

Scotland

One summer morning, a fox was trotting through the woods beside the green waters of the loch. He looked this way and that, hoping to find a juicy bite of breakfast. Out on the water, among the reeds, a duck was swimming. 'There's as fine a breakfast as I could hope for,' thought the fox, 'but, alas, beyond my reach.'

'Good morning to you, Mr Duck!' the fox called out.

'You go away, Fox!' quacked the duck in alarm.

'I only said good morning,' said the fox. 'There's no reason to be rude.'

'I know your kind!' scoffed Mr Duck, 'and I never speak to fellows like you. I've seen you chasing us ducks. And you gobble us up when you can catch us! No, I've no interest in talking to you. Good day!'

'Forgive me for startling you. I meant you no harm,' said the fox. 'I only wished to tell you of the shocking scandal about your neighbour, Mrs Goose. I

know you dearly love a juicy bit of gossip. But I'm sure you have already heard of it and that is why you are so upset. Good day to you, Mr Duck.' And the fox turned as if to leave.

'Wait a moment,' said Mr Duck. 'I haven't heard. Tell me about it.'

The fox looked around. 'I'm afraid the story is too shocking to tell in a loud voice. I don't want her to overhear, you see. I'm surprised you haven't heard it yet. Everyone around here knows.'

Mr Duck shook his head. 'Please tell me,' he said eagerly.

'Very well,' said the fox. 'Come closer and I'll tell you.'

Mr Duck swam closer. 'You say it's *very* shocking?' he said.

'Why, it's the juiciest piece of gossip I've heard all week. I'm afraid you'll have to come closer so that I can whisper it in your ear.'

Mr Duck swam quickly toward the fox, but as soon as he was within reach, the fox seized him and ate him up in a few quick bites.

After he had finished his breakfast, the fox trotted happily into the woods, brushing the feathers from his red coat. 'Yes, it was a juicy tale indeed, Mr Duck,' he sighed, patting his full belly. 'Mrs Goose loved gossip as much as you did — she was my breakfast yesterday.'

Vanya and the Rabbit

Russia

Once there was a farmer named Vanya. One day, as he was standing in his potato field, he saw a big brown rabbit nibbling at the weeds in a ditch.

'Ha!' thought Vanya. 'What good fortune has come to me! I will set a snare and trap that rabbit and sell him in the market-place for ten kopeks. With those ten kopeks, I shall buy myself a nice sow which will give me ten piglets. I shall sell my ten piglets and then I shall have enough money to buy a cow. With the money I get when I sell the cow, I shall be a rich man. Then I shall get married.

'My wife and I will have three sons, Misha, Grisha, and Sasha. When the boys grow up, they will work on the farm too. They'll be good sons, but I'll have to watch them closely to see that they work hard.

'"Misha, Grisha, and Sasha!" I'll scold them, "Plough that furrow straight! You lazy boys, how do you expect to become good farmers if you don't do your work?"'

But Vanya shouted these words and startled the rabbit. It bolted into the weeds and disappeared. And with it went all Vanya's dreams — including Misha, Grisha, and Sasha.

Tutokanula

Miwok (California)

Two boys lived in the Yosemite Valley. One day they went down to the river to swim. They swam and played in the water until they were tired. Then they climbed onto a large, flat rock to dry themselves in the sunshine. It was very warm, and soon they fell asleep. Nothing woke them.

They slept through moons and snows, through winter and summer. Little by little, the big rock they slept on began to grow taller. After a time, the rock had risen very high. Their friends searched for the two boys, but they could not find them. Still the rock kept rising. It rose up into the clouds. It rose until they almost scraped themselves on the moon. Still nothing woke them. They slept on.

The animals came to try to bring them down from there. One by one, they tried to spring up the smooth rock face. The little gray mouse tried, but it could only jump a short way. Next came the rat, but it could only jump a little farther than the mouse. The racoon tried,

and it jumped farther than the rat, but not far enough. The grizzly bear tried, and it made a mighty leap, but it still fell far short of the top. Then came the mountain lion. It sprang up high, higher than any of the other animals. But it could not reach the top of the high rock.

Last came Tultakana, the tiny inch-worm, so small that even the mouse could have stepped on it and crushed it. The inch-worm began to creep up the rock. One inch at a time, the worm climbed. It climbed higher than the little gray mouse had jumped. It climbed higher than the rat had jumped. It climbed higher than the racoon had jumped. It climbed higher than the grizzly bear had jumped. It climbed higher than the mountain lion had jumped. And still it climbed. It crawled up till it was beyond sight of the other animals. Through many sleeps, for one whole snow, it crawled, all the way up to the clouds. At last it reached the top. It woke the boys, and they climbed down to the ground. So the people called the great rock Tutokanula after Tultakana, the little inch-worm.

How Anansi became a Spider

Dagomba (Togo)

In West Africa, they tell many stories about Anansi. Some call him other names, such as Kwaku Ananse or Gizo. He is also known in the West Indies, the southern United States, and Surinam — wherever there are people whose ancestors came from West Africa. A clever and wily fellow, Anansi appears as a man in some stories and as a spider in others. Sometimes he can turn himself into a spider to escape danger. He is always trying to outwit other animals and man, but sometimes Anansi's schemes go awry. This story tells how Anansi became a spider.

Long ago, Anansi and his family lived in the same compound as a hunter and his family. Now, it happened that hard times came to the household, and food was scarce. Every day the hunter went to the bush, but he could find no animals for meat. Day after day, he returned empty-handed. Anansi also searched for food, with no better luck.

One day, the hunter said, 'I shall go into the far bush. Perhaps there I shall find an antelope so that my family will have meat.' He walked and walked, farther than he had ever gone before. After a time, he became tired and stopped to rest. He sat under a large, shady tree and fell asleep.

Suddenly a sound awakened him. He looked around and saw that there on the ground was a tiny mat which had not been there before. But the hunter did not move. He just watched. Soon he saw a tiny pillow fall from a branch high above him. It landed on top of the tiny mat. Next, out of the tree dropped a tiny man — a forest gnome.

'Have you any food by chance?' the gnome asked the hunter.

'I'm sorry,' said the hunter, 'I have very little food. But what I have I will share with you.'

After they had eaten, the gnome asked the hunter to carry him down to the river nearby. The hunter picked up the tiny man and placed him on his shoulder. He carried him to the river and set him down on the bank.

'There are tasty fish in the river,' said the gnome. 'Would you like to have some?'

'I would!' said the man. 'But I am a hunter and I have nothing with which to catch them.'

'No matter,' said the gnome. 'I will help you.'

'Thank you,' said the hunter politely, though he wondered just how the gnome could be of any help catching fish in the swift river.

'Take all the fish you want,' said the tiny man, and bent down to take a drink from the river. He drank and drank and drank and did not stop drinking until he had swallowed the whole river. Now that the water was gone, the fish could not swim away. They lay flapping about on the dry river bed. The large animals, crocodiles and hippopotamuses, lay on the sand and did not move.

The hunter lost no time. He went into the river bed and gathered up as many fish as he could, throwing them out onto the bank. He took all the fish he thought he and his family could eat. Soon he saw that the gnome could no longer hold back the water, so he climbed out of the river bed. As soon as he was on the bank, the gnome opened his mouth. The river water poured back into its bed and soon the river was running as swiftly as ever.

After thanking the gnome for the fish, the hunter picked up the tiny man and took him back to the tree.

'I shall always remember your kindness in sharing your food with me,' said the gnome. 'If ever you should find yourself in need again, come to me. You

shall have all the fish you require.'

Then the hunter went back to the river. He gathered up the fish and took them home.

Anansi watched the hunter as he came into the compound. 'Where did you get so many fish?' cried Anansi.

'I went far, far into the bush and saw wonderful things,' said the hunter. 'The fish were given to me.'

But Anansi, who was quick-tempered, became angry. 'Why didn't you ask me to go with you?' he cried. 'I am known as a great fisherman. I could have brought back many times more fish!'

'Next time, you shall go with me,' said the hunter.

In a few days, all the fish were eaten, and the hunter decided to go out again to find food for his family. He took Anansi along. The two friends went far back into the bush. Along their way, they killed a small antelope. They sat under a tree, made a fire, and began to cook the meat. Suddenly a sound startled Anansi, and he jumped. But the hunter paid no attention. The tiny mat fell out of the tree onto the ground beside them. Anansi cried in alarm, 'What is that? Let us go away from here!'

But the hunter calmly continued cooking the meat. Then the tiny pillow fell down onto the tiny mat. Anansi became alarmed again, but the hunter acted as if nothing were wrong. Then the gnome himself dropped down out of the tree onto the mat.

When Anansi saw the strange little man, he laughed unkindly. 'So,' he said, 'it was only you making all that noise. Go away, and don't bother us here. We are busy, you see.'

The gnome spoke to Anansi. 'May I have some of that meat you are cooking?'

'No!' said Anansi.

But the hunter said, 'Please share our food with us,' and gave the little man some antelope meat.

'Why have you come back, hunter?' said the gnome. 'Did you not have enough fish?'

'My family ate all the fish,' answered the hunter. 'I remembered your promise and have brought my friend Anansi, whose family is also hungry.'

The gnome said to Anansi, 'Since you are his friend and he has brought you out of kindness, I will ignore your bad manners. Let us go to the river.' The hunter then took up the gnome and placed him on his shoulder as before. At this, Anansi laughed.

'Carry him about if you like,' he said, 'but I am no slave to carry little men on my back.'

Soon the three arrived at the river.

'Do you like fish?' the gnome asked Anansi.

'Yes, of course,' he snapped. 'But how can we catch them?'

'I shall help you,' said the gnome.

The hunter thanked the little man, but Anansi laughed rudely.

'You?' he scoffed. 'Ha-ha-ha! And how shall you help us?'

'Take as much fish as you need, hunter,' said the gnome.

The tiny man bent down and began to drink the water of the river. He drank and drank and drank and did not stop drinking until the river bed was dry. As before, there were many fish flapping about on the sand and crocodiles and hippopotamuses lying here and there. Anansi was astonished.

But while the hunter gathered up fish, Anansi did not gather any fish at all. Instead he busied himself with the crocodiles and hippopotamuses, throwing them out onto the bank.

'Why bother with fish when you can have meat?' Anansi said to the hunter. But the hunter kept gathering fish.

At last the hunter saw that the gnome could no longer hold back the river, and he told Anansi to hurry and climb out. Just as they reached the bank, the gnome opened his mouth and the river water rushed out. Soon the river was running in its course just as before.

The hunter thanked the gnome and carried him back to his tree. Anansi said nothing. He went off into the bush to make some rope so he could tie up the animals he had taken from the river. Anansi made a lot of rope. When he came back, and the animals saw him, they got up and walked back into the river. But the fish that the hunter had gathered were still lying on the bank.

Anansi saw how foolish he had been. The hunter went home with many fish, but Anansi returned to his family without anything at all. So ashamed was he that he hid in the dark corners of the house and would not come out. And that is why even now Anansi always hides himself and keeps to the dark corners in the house of his friend, Man.

The Luckiest Woman in the World

England

Once upon a time there was a poor old woman who made her living by doing odd jobs and running errands for the farmers' wives in her village. Although she did not earn much, with a bit of porridge at one house and a few potatoes at another, and a cup of tea at yet a third, she never went hungry and always looked as cheerful as if she were the luckiest woman in the world.

One summer evening as she was walking home, she stumbled on a big black pot in the middle of the road. Instead of cursing her sore toes, she was delighted with her find. 'That old pot would be perfect to put something into,' she said, 'if I had anything to put into it. I wonder whose it is?' She looked all about, but she could see no one to whom the pot might belong.

'Perhaps it has a hole in it,' she said, 'and that's why it has been thrown here in the road. If it has a

hole in it, it would make a fine flower pot, wouldn't it?' And she bent down to look inside.

'Mercy me!' she cried, jumping back in surprise. 'If it isn't brim-full of gold coins! Aren't I the luckiest woman in the world?'

She tied one end of her shawl to a handle of the pot and began to drag it along after her.

After a while, she stopped to rest. The pot was heavy, and she still had a long way to go. But when she looked back, she saw that tied to her shawl there wasn't a pot of gold coins at all but a big lump of silver. She rubbed her eyes and stared at it, but it still looked like a lump of silver. At last she shook her head.

'I was sure it was a pot of gold,' she said, 'but my eyes must have been playing tricks on me. This is all for the better, for silver is less trouble to look after and less easily stolen. It would have been a bother to take care of all those gold coins, now, wouldn't it? I'm well rid of them. Aren't I the luckiest woman in the world?'

She set off again toward home. It wasn't long before the old woman became tired once more and stopped to rest. When she looked back at her treasure, she gasped in surprise. 'Land sakes! It's turned into a lump of iron! Well, I can sell a lump of iron just as easily as silver, and I'll get a lot of pennies for it. After all, a lump of silver would have been quite a bother.

No, a piece of iron is a very useful thing to have.' And the old woman went on her way, dragging the lump of iron behind her.

After a while, she looked over her shoulder to check on her fine piece of iron, but as soon as she set eyes on it, she cried out, 'Oh my! If it hasn't turned into a great big stone! Well, isn't that lucky? I'm terribly in need of a doorstop. And what a fine doorstop this stone will make. Aren't I the luckiest woman in the world?' Cheerful as ever, she went on her way.

Soon she reached her own little gate. As she stooped to untie her shawl from the stone, the stone began to change. Before her eyes, it grew as big as a horse. It stood up on four long legs and shook its long ears. Then, swishing its tail to and fro, it galloped away down the lane, neighing and laughing and kicking its legs in the air.

The old woman stared after it until it disappeared into the darkness. 'My stars!' she said. 'Just imagine my seeing such a wondrous, magical creature as that all by myself, right in front of my own front gate! All the gold and silver in the kingdom couldn't buy such a sight!'

She gathered up her shawl from the dust and went into her cottage and sat down by the hearth. 'Aren't I the luckiest woman in the world?' she sighed.

The Quarrelling Quail

India

Once, thousands of quail lived in a forest. Whenever their leader wanted to summon them, it gave a special call, and the quail flocked together.

Near the forest lived a man who caught and sold quail for a living. Every day he listened to the leader calling the quail, and after a time he learned to imitate the leader's call very cleverly. He hid himself behind a tree and called the birds, just as their leader did. When the quail heard that familiar sound, they thought it was their leader calling them, and they gathered together.

Quickly the fowler stepped out of his hiding place and threw his net over them, capturing as many as he could. Then he crammed the quail into his basket and took them to market.

One day, the leader of the quail called all the birds together and said to them, 'If we do not do something, this fowler will carry off every one of us! Listen to me, my good quail, for I have a plan. The next time

he throws his net over us, each quail must put its head through a hole in the net. Then we must fly away together until we find a thorn bush. We will leave the net on the thorns, free ourselves, and fly away.'

The quail agreed that this was a wonderful plan, and they promised to do what their leader had told them to.

The next day, the fowler came to the forest again. He hid behind a tree and imitated the leader's call. All the quail flocked together and the fowler hurled his net over them. They were trapped. But they remembered the words of their leader, and each bird put its head through a hole in the net. Together they lifted the net and flew off. They flew until they found a thorn bush, where they left the net and freed themselves.

The fowler spent the rest of the day searching for his net, and by the time he untangled it from the thorns, evening had come. That night he returned home without a single quail in his basket.

The next day, when the fowler went to the forest, the same thing happened. And the day after, the quail outsmarted the fowler once more. The fowler now spent the days not catching quail, but searching for his net and untangling it from the thorns. Every night he went home empty-handed.

'The fact is,' he said to himself, 'those quail are working together. As soon as I throw my net over them, off they fly with it and leave it on a thorn bush. But sooner or later they will begin to quarrel, and then I shall catch them all.'

One day, not long afterwards, one of the quail accidentally stepped on another quail's head as they were landing on their feeding ground.

'Who stepped on my head?' cried the second quail.

'I did, but I didn't mean to,' said the first. 'Don't be angry.'

But the second quail said, 'You clumsy bird! Watch where you land.'

'Clumsy? I suppose you lift the net by yourself?'

'Well, to tell the truth, you aren't much help!' And soon all the quail were quarrelling among themselves.

It was not long before the fowler came to the forest again. As he had done before, he hid behind a tree and imitated the leader's call. As they always did when they heard that call, the quail gathered together. The fowler hurled his net over them. But this time, instead of lifting the net, one quail said to another, 'They say that when you try to lift the net your feathers fall out. Now's your chance to show how strong you are, lift away!'

And the other said, 'They say you don't even try to lift the net. Now's your chance, lift away!'

Another bird cried, 'You birds over there don't

help a bit. We over here do all the work lifting the net!'

And the other birds answered, 'It is we who do all the work; you birds just pretend to lift the net!'

While the quail were quarrelling about who should lift the net, the fowler himself lifted it, and shook out the birds into his basket. He took them to market and sold them all, and for a good price too.

Coyote and Woodpecker

Pueblo (New Mexico)

Coyote and his family lived near a forest. In the forest was a great old hollow tree, and Woodpecker and his family lived there. One day, as Coyote was walking, he met Woodpecker.

'How are you today, my friend?' said Coyote.

'Very well, thank you,' replied Woodpecker. 'And how are you?'

They talked together for a while. Then Coyote said, 'Friend Woodpecker, bring your wife and children tonight and join my family for supper.'

'Thank you, friend Coyote,' said Woodpecker. 'We will gladly come.'

That evening, Woodpecker and his family went to the coyotes' home. They fluttered to the ground and then, as they always do after flying, the woodpeckers stretched themselves. As they lifted their wings, the coyotes could see their pretty red and yellow feathers underneath. And as the woodpeckers ate supper,

whenever they raised their wings, their bright feathers could be seen.

After the woodpeckers had eaten, they thanked their host politely. 'Please come to our house tomorrow for supper, friend Coyote,' said Woodpecker. And Coyote said yes, he and his family certainly would.

After the woodpeckers left, Coyote turned to his family and said, 'Did you see how those woodpeckers showed off their bright red and yellow feathers? No doubt they think they are more beautiful than we are, and they want to be sure we know it. Well, we will show them that coyotes are just as beautiful as woodpeckers.'

The next day, Coyote made all his family work hard gathering many loads of fire wood. When evening came, he built a big fire and called his family there. He tied a burning stick to each of them, under their arms, so that the burning end pointed forward. Then he did the same to himself. 'Now we coyotes will show those woodpeckers who has beautiful colours!' he told his family. 'And don't you forget to raise your arms often, to be sure they see we are just as good as they are!' Then the coyotes went to the woodpeckers' house.

When they came to the hollow tree, Woodpecker welcomed them and invited them in very politely. Together, the woodpecker family and the coyote family sat down to supper. As they ate, the coyotes kept raising their arms to show the bright fire underneath. But suddenly one of Coyote's sons yelled, 'Ayee! My fire is burning me, papa!'

'Hush!' said Coyote, 'Don't give us away.'

'Ah!' sighed one of Coyote's daughters, 'My fire is out!' This was too much for Coyote, and he scolded her.

Then Woodpecker spoke. 'Tell me, Friend Coyote,' he said, 'why is it that your colours are bright red and yellow at first but later become ash gray?'

'Oh, that,' said Coyote, smiling pleasantly although he was very angry inside. 'That is the best thing about our colours, for they do not stay the same — as other people's do — but turn many shades.'

Coyote made an excuse so that he and his family could leave, for they were all smarting from their burns.

After they left, Woodpecker gathered his family around and said, 'Now, my children, you have seen what Coyote has tried to do. Never pretend to be what you are not. Always be just what you really are, and you will never need to put on false colours.'

The Wondrous Pillow

China

Once, long ago, in old China, a young farmer named Chen stopped at an inn along the road to have a bowl of millet porridge. An old man entered the inn and sat down beside him, and soon the two were talking and laughing together as they drank their tea.

Suddenly Chen looked down at himself and said, 'How miserable my life is!'

'You don't look miserable to me,' said the old man. 'We were having such an enjoyable talk — why do you suddenly complain that you are miserable? Are you not content with your life?'

'How can I be content,' said Chen, 'when I must work from dawn till nightfall? Now, if I were a wealthy man and wore rich silks and had servants to do my work for me, then I would certainly be content!'

The old man thought for a moment. Then he said, 'So much talk can easily make one sleepy. Don't you want to lie down and rest awhile?'

'I *am* rather sleepy,' said Chen, and in fact he

could barely speak those words between yawns. 'I think I shall rest until my millet porridge is ready.'

The old man reached into his bag and brought out a kind of pillow made of glazed porcelain. It was oblong in shape and curved inward in the middle. A flowery design showed through its delicate greenish-blue glaze, and there was a small round hole in one of the ends. It was hollow.

'Rest your head upon this awhile, young man,' he said, 'and find your wish granted.'

As Chen put his head down, he noticed something curious inside the small hole at the end of the pillow. He bent to look closer and found that he could easily crawl right inside. He did, and found himself in the lane outside his own home. Nothing seemed changed. But when he stepped inside the door of his house, he saw piles of gold and silver all around. He had never seen so much wealth in all his life.

'That old man must have been a magician,' he thought, 'and he has granted my wish and given me wealth so that I may be contented. How can I ever thank him?'

Chen began to gather up the gold and silver, but there was so much that he didn't know where to put it. 'It certainly would not do to leave such riches lying about in a simple country house without any locks on the doors,' said Chen to himself. 'Besides, now that I am a wealthy man, I need no longer live in this hovel.'

He looked around at his little house with its plain wood doors and its simple table and chair. 'A man so rich as I should have the finest lacquered tables, the rarest porcelain vases and the most delicate of carved jades. Naturally I shall need a palace to keep all my treasures in,' he said. 'With tall stone gates too,' he added.

Soon Chen had his palace. And it was perched on top of a hill, for Chen did not think it proper to build such a magnificent place too close to the simple country homes of his neighbours.

'A man so wealthy as I should not be seen with those poor peasants,' he said. So he shut himself up in his palace with its rare porcelain vases, fine lacquered tables, delicate carved jades — and tall stone gates.

But Chen found himself pacing the grounds restlessly. 'Something is not quite right,' he said. 'What is it? I know. It's too plain around here. This place needs flowers and trees and ponds with fish in them.' So he ordered gardens and fishponds put in.

Still Chen found himself wandering aimlessly among the trees and flowering bushes. The sound of water filling the ponds did nothing to soothe him.

'Something else is missing,' he said. 'I know. It's too quiet. This place needs musicians and singers to play lively music and sing cheerful songs.' So Chen ordered that musicians and singers come to the palace.

But soon Chen found all that music and song tiresome, and he finally told them all to leave. For although they followed him about all day long, singing and playing the moon guitar and the flute, they never talked to him. Having them around made him feel terribly lonely.

'What I need is a companion, a wife. That's it: that's what is missing from my life!' said Chen to himself. So he sent word around that, early the next morning, all the unmarried young women in the village should come to the gates of the palace, and he would choose one of them to be his wife.

But when the next day dawned, there was no one at the gates.

'Ungrateful peasants!' snorted Chen. 'I'm better off alone.' But still he felt something was missing.

One morning, he was sitting in his room on the top floor of his palace, surrounded by his porcelains and his jades. He looked out the window at the green patches of field beside the road that led to the village. A group of soldiers walked along the road. Beside them on horseback rode their commander. He sat up straight and proud and wore so many plumes and so much fine armour that he looked very fearsome indeed.

'I have it!' shouted Chen, pounding his fist on the lacquered table before him. 'What I need is power. If I had my own army, then I'd be content. I'd be able to make everyone else do what I tell them. Why, I'd be able to cast down the Emperor and sit on his throne myself. I'd be ruler of all China. Then I'd make these country folk tremble. Yes, that would make me a happy man indeed.'

So Chen began to gather his army. He sent word through the land that any man who wanted to soldier for him would earn a string of bronze coins every day, which was a great deal more than the Emperor paid them.

Word reached the Emperor that one of his subjects was gathering an army. The Emperor knew that one only gathers a private army for a single reason, so he knew that Chen intended to take the throne for himself. Before Chen could get ten men together, the Emperor sent soldiers to arrest him for treason.

The soldiers took Chen to the capital to be executed. On the way, they passed the inn by the side of the road. Chen looked inside and saw the men of the village laughing and talking and drinking their tea and eating their millet porridge. And he sighed.

When they arrived at the place of execution, they made Chen kneel while the executioner stood over him, his blade shining in the sun. As he raised the sword, Chen shut his eyes.

But when he opened them again, he saw that he was still at the inn. He sat up quickly. Beside him was the old man, drinking his tea with a thoughtful look on his face. The innkeeper was just spooning Chen's millet porridge into a bowl. Chen took the bowl and ate his millet porridge in silence. It tasted more delicious than the rarest delicacy. After he finished it, he stood up and bowed to the old man.

'I thank you, old sir,' he said, 'for lending me your wondrous pillow. It has taught me that the greatest treasure of all is contentment.'

And with that, he went back to his work.

Clever Jackal

Khoi-Khoi (South Africa)

One night Jackal went to the kraal where the lambs were kept. He went in and stole a fat lamb. Next night, he stole another. Every night Jackal crept into the kraal and took a lamb. One night he came again. But now a snare was set for him. Jackal stepped on the stick. Zip — it pulled the noose around his body, and he found himself swinging in the air. He could not reach the ground. Night passed and day began to dawn. Jackal was worried.

Monkey sat on a stone wall and watched. 'Ha-ha-ha, Jackal, so at last there you are — caught.'

'What?' said Jackal. 'You are mistaken. I am swinging for fun. I enjoy it.'

'You fibber,' said Monkey. 'You are caught in the trap.'

'I caught in a trap? Oh, not at all. Foolish Monkey! If only you knew how lovely and relaxing it is to swing in the air, you would do so yourself every day. Would you like to try it for a while?'

'No!' said Monkey. 'I can see that you are caught.'

'Then, don't try it,' said Jackal. 'I shall enjoy myself and you shall miss all the fun.' Jackal began to sway this way and that, singing to himself. 'Oh, my! What fun! He-he-he, ah, me!'

After a while Monkey sprang down from the wall. 'Let me try it,' he said.

'What? You?' said Jackal. 'Well, just once. And only for a short while.'

Monkey freed Jackal and climbed into the noose. Then Jackal let go the stick and — zip! Now it was Monkey who was swinging in the air. He screeched and screamed. But Jackal laughed.

'Now you are caught.'

'Free me!' cried Monkey. 'This is no fun at all!'

'I'm afraid I cannot,' said Jackal, 'for I hear someone coming. I must leave now. But you stay and enjoy yourself. It was your wish to swing.' And Jackal ran away.

The Flight of the Animals

Tibet

Once long ago, beside a lake, there stood a forest which was home to a family of hares. One day a large, ripe fruit fell from one of the trees into the lake, hitting the water with a loud PLOP! At this sudden noise, the frightened hares began to scamper off as fast as they could go.

They came to the monkeys. 'Why are you running?' asked the monkeys.

'Plop is coming!' cried the hares. 'Run for your life!' And the monkeys began to run as fast as they could, following the hares.

They came to the gazelles. 'Why do you run away?' asked the gazelles.

'Haven't you heard?' shrieked the monkeys. 'Plop is coming! Run for your life!' And the gazelles bounded away with the others.

They came to the bears. 'Where are you going?'

asked the bears.

'Haven't you heard?' called the gazelles. 'Plop is coming! Run for your life!' And the bears began to run too.

They came to the jackals. 'Why are you fleeing?' asked the jackals.

'Haven't you heard?' bellowed the bears. 'Plop is coming! Run for your life!' And the jackals leaped to their feet and joined the stampede.

They came to the tigers. 'What are you running from?' asked the tigers.

'Haven't you heard?' howled the jackals. 'Plop is coming! Run for your life!' And the tigers sprang up and began to run with the rest.

At last the frightened animals came to an old lion with a great golden mane. 'Why are you animals running away?' said the lion.

'Haven't you heard?' roared the tigers. 'Plop is coming! Run for your life!'

'Who is Plop?' said the lion. 'Did any of you tigers see him?'

'No,' said the tigers. 'The jackals told us.'

'Did any of you jackals see him?'

'No,' said the jackals. 'The bears told us.'

'Then, did any of you bears see him?'

'No,' said the bears. 'The gazelles told us.'

'Well, did any of you gazelles see him?'

'No,' said the gazelles. 'The monkeys told us.'

'Then, did any of you monkeys see him?'

'No,' said the monkeys. 'The hares told us.'

'Well, then, did any of you hares see him?'

'No,' said the hares, 'but we heard him. All of us heard Plop with our very own ears.'

'Let us go back to the place where you heard this Plop,' said the lion. Together the animals followed the hares to the forest beside the lake. As they stood there, another ripe fruit fell into the lake with a loud PLOP!

'There is your fearsome Plop!' said the lion. 'Foolish animals! If I had not stopped you, you might still be running away from nothing at all.'

Smells and Jingles

Japan

In old Japan, there lived an old woman who loved to eat broiled eels. And how lucky for her, for she lived next door to the eel-seller's shop. During the night, the eel-seller caught his eels, and in the daytime he served them, smoking hot, to his customers. He cut the eels into pieces three or four inches long and cooked them on a griddle over red hot charcoal until they were ready to eat.

Although she dearly loved eels, the old woman could not afford to buy them as often as she liked, and when she was short of money she would take her bowl of rice and sit close to her neighbour's door. Eating her boiled rice, and sniffing the aroma of the broiled eels, she enjoyed with her nose what she could not pay for to put in her mouth.

When the eel-seller found this out, he became quite angry and thought he would charge his neighbour for the smell of the eels. So, he made out his bill and presented it gruffly to the old woman. But she

only smiled. She brought out her iron money-box, which at that time was nearly empty. But it doesn't take many coins in a moneybox to make a good jingle. The woman shook the money-box in the eel-seller's face. 'Did you hear that, neighbour?'

'Indeed I did!' he said.

'Then we are even,' said the woman, with a bow.

'What?' cried the eel-seller. 'Aren't you going to pay me?'

'I have paid you,' said the woman. 'You have charged me for the smell of eels, and I have paid you with the sound of money.'

The Mouse and the Mountain

Eskimo

Once there was a little mouse who was very proud of himself. One day while he was sleeping in a corner, a noise woke him up. He saw that a bright fire was burning at the doorway.

'What shall I do?' he said. 'If I stay here, I shall certainly be burnt up. I have no choice but to try to run through those terrible, bright flames.' The little mouse ran as fast as he could. He ran straight through the doorway, but he was not burnt at all.

'What a great mouse I am,' he said. 'Not even fire can burn me!' And he felt very proud of himself. Then he looked at the fire again and saw that the bright fire was not fire at all. It was only sunshine.

'How silly of me!' said the little mouse. 'Now how can I prove I am great?'

The mouse looked about. He saw a high hill. 'That must be the highest hill in the world. I know what I

shall do. I will leap over it. Then all shall know how great I am.'

The mouse jumped as high as he could. He landed on the other side of the hill. 'What a great mouse I am,' he said. 'I can jump the highest hill!' And he felt very proud of himself indeed. But when he looked again, he saw that the high hill was not a hill at all. It was only a small mound of sand.

'How foolish of me,' said the little mouse. 'I shall have to find some other way to show that I am great.'

The mouse looked about again. He saw a big lake. 'That must be the widest lake in the world,' he said. 'I know what I shall do. I will swim across it. Then I shall be great.'

The little mouse walked toward the lake. He walked for a long time, and at last he reached the shore. The lake was so wide that he could not even see the other side.

The mouse began to swim. It took him a long time to cross the lake. When he crawled out of the water, he was very tired. 'What a great mouse I am,' he said, 'I can swim the widest lake!' Then the mouse looked at the lake again and saw that the wide lake was not a lake at all. It was only a mud puddle.

'What a silly mistake,' said the mouse. 'Now what can I do to prove I am great?'

The mouse looked about. He saw a tall tree. 'That must be the tallest tree in the world,' he said. 'If I cut down that tall tree, then all shall call me great.'

The mouse walked and walked and at last he came to the foot of the tree. He began to gnaw at the tree with his teeth. The tree was so tall that he could not see the top. At last it began to fall. It hit the earth with a crash.

'What a great mouse I am,' he said. 'I can cut down the tallest tree!' And the little mouse was very proud of himself. But the mouse looked at the tree again and saw that the tall tree was not a tree at all. It was only a blade of grass.

'Shame on me!' said the little mouse. 'I thought sunshine was fire. I thought a sand heap was a hill. I thought a mud puddle was a lake. I thought a blade of grass was a tall tree. I am not great at all. I am a small and silly mouse.'

Across the tundra, the little mouse saw a great mountain. 'I am so small I could only carry a single grain of sand from that great mountain,' he said.

The mouse walked and walked and at last he arrived at the mountain. He took up one grain of sand in his little paws. He carried the grain of sand across the tundra. Then he went back to the mountain and carried another grain of sand. Day after day, the little mouse carried one grain of sand at a time. At last the day came when there were no more grains of sand left. The little mouse had carried the great mountain across the tundra.

The Goose and the Moon

Iran

A goose was searching for fish one night when she saw the new moon's reflection on the quiet pond.

'A fish!' she said, and dived into the water. But she found no fish.

When the ripples went away and the water grew still, the silvery reflection of the moon came back.

'A fish!' cried the goose happily, and dived into the water again. But again she caught nothing. When the pond became calm once more, the reflection of the moon floated on the dark water.

'A fish?' said the goose. But when she dived into the water, once more she found nothing.

'Where is that fish?' she thought angrily. Then she looked up and saw the new moon shining in the sky.

'So that's it,' she grumbled. 'It was only the moon reflected on the water of the pond. But it shall not fool me again!' And off she went.

The next night, the goose went back to the pond. A silvery fish was swimming just below the surface of the water. The goose turned up her beak and shook her feathers in disgust. 'That moon again! But I'm a wise goose now — it doesn't fool me!' And she waddled off to hunt for worms in the mud.

The Tortoise that talked too much

India

Once upon a time, in a green pond in the jungle, there lived a little green tortoise. Two wild ducks often came to the pond to look for food, and they became good friends with the tortoise. All day long, while they searched for food, the little tortoise talked and talked. There was nothing he liked more than to talk, and he talked to anyone who would listen.

One day, it was time for the ducks to fly back to their home. 'Friend Tortoise,' said one of the ducks, 'our home high in the mountains of Himalaya is a beautiful place. There is a lovely clear pond and many good things to eat. You would be very happy there. Will you come with us to visit our home?'

'I would like that very much,' said the tortoise, 'but how would I get there? I cannot fly.'

'We will take you,' said the other duck. 'My brother and I shall take a stick in our mouths. You

shall hold onto the middle of the stick with your teeth, and together the three of us will fly away to the mountains. But, on the journey, you must promise not to speak to anyone at all.'

'I can easily do that,' said the little green tortoise. 'If that is all there is to it, I shall certainly go with you.'

The two ducks found a stick. The tortoise held onto the middle of it with his teeth, while the ducks took the ends in their mouths. They flew up into the sky and soon the little green pond was just a tiny speck far below.

They flew over the rice fields where the villagers were working. The people looked up and saw the tortoise being carried through the air by the ducks.

'Look!' said one of them. 'A tortoise is flying away with two ducks! Where can he be going?'

The tortoise heard and wanted to answer, 'I am going with my friends to their home high in the mountains of Himalaya,' but he had promised not to say a word, so he kept silent.

'How clever the tortoise is!' said one of the villagers. 'He flies through the air and lets the ducks do all the work carrying him!' The ducks paid no attention at all to those words and flew on, just as before. But the tortoise felt very proud. How clever he was to let his friends carry him through the air!

They flew over the village where the children were

playing. 'Look!' said one of the children. 'What clever ducks! They found a way to carry a tortoise through the air!' As before, the ducks ignored what was said and kept on flying. But the tortoise's pride was hurt. 'I'm just as clever as they are!' he shouted.

But, of course, as soon as he opened his mouth to speak, he lost hold of the stick. He fell straight down to the ground, and that was the end of him.

'Poor little tortoise,' said one of the ducks, looking down at him. 'He could not keep silent.'

Many Ears of Corn

Maya (Mexico)

Long ago, when the world was young and the animals could talk, there lived in the land of Mayab a people called the Maya. Although much has changed in the world since those days, the Maya still live in that land, but it is now called Yucatan. And much of the way they live is still the same as it was then.

In those days, the Maya lived in houses made of wood poles with mud walls and roofs of thatch, just as they do today. They called the white corn, or maize, *zac ishim* and beans *buul* and chiles *ic*, and they ate corn tortillas called *wah* at every meal, just as they do now. Corn was precious to the Maya and still is. Corn gave the Maya life, so they were careful not to waste it.

Each morning the Mayan women prepared enough tortillas for the day's meals. First they separated the dry kernels of corn from the cob, then they boiled the corn in a pot with lime. When the corn was soft, they ground it on a large stone called *ka* with the handstone called *u-kab-ka* to make a dough. They patted out

some dough with their hands into a flat, round tortilla — *wah* — and cooked the tortilla on a flat pan called *shamach*. When the tortillas were cooked, they were kept warm in a hollow dried gourd called a *lec*. This is still the way the Mayan women make their delicious tortillas today.

But in those long-ago, magical times, the Mayan women were very lucky for they only had to use one ear of corn to make enough tortillas for a whole day. Even though it was not difficult to do, there was one young Mayan girl who did not like to make tortillas at all. She did not like to help her mother separate the kernels of corn from the cob. She did not like to put the corn in a pot to boil. She did not like to grind the softened corn on the large stone. She did not even like to pat the dough with her hands to make the tortillas, or cook them on the *shamach*. She only liked to eat the tortillas that her mother made, and then run off to play.

One day the girl's mother said to her, 'I must go on an errand now. While I am gone you must prepare the tortillas just as I have shown you. Remember that you must only use one ear of corn.' Then she went off.

The girl brought out the clay pot and snapped the dried kernels off one ear of corn, just as she had seen her mother do every day. After she put the corn into the pot, she said to herself, 'If I put in another ear of corn, it will make enough tortillas for today and tomorrow, and then I will not have to work for a whole day!' So she put in the kernels from a second ear of corn.

Then she said to herself, 'If I put another ear of corn into the pot, it will make enough tortillas for today and tomorrow and the day after tomorrow, and then I will not have to work for two days!' So she put in a third ear of corn.

Then she said to herself, 'If I put in many ears of corn, it will make enough tortillas to last forever, and then I will never have to work again!' So she snapped off the dried kernels from many ears of corn, and she put them all into the clay pot.

Now the pot was so heavy that she could hardly lift it onto the fire. '*There!*' she said. 'Very good. It will take a long time for all that corn to cook.' So she went off to play.

When she came back, she looked into the pot. But although the fire was still burning under it, and everything else was just as she had left it, in the pot there was exactly the same amount as there had been when her mother had used just one ear of corn. There was still only enough for one day's tortillas.

Time passed and the world grew older and less magical, and the animals forgot how to talk. And ever since that day, the Mayan women have had to work very hard and boil many ears of corn every day in order to make enough tortillas for their families to eat.

The Magic Tree

Russia

Once upon a time, in a small hut near the forest there lived a man and his wife. One day the man went to the forest to chop down a tree for firewood. He chose a fine, tall tree and raised his axe to strike. But before he could land the blow, a voice spoke to him.

'Stop!' it cried. 'Let me live, my good man. Please do not chop me down.'

'What's this?' he said. 'A tree that talks?' and he hurried home to tell his wife.

'Surely it was a magic tree,' she said. 'Why didn't you ask it to grant you a wish? Go back, right away, and ask it to give us a nice cottage instead of this poor hut.'

The man went back to the forest to find the tree. He raised his axe as if to strike it.

'What do you want?' asked the tree.

'My wife and I wish to have a nice cottage to live in instead of our poor hut.'

'It is already done,' said the tree.

And when the man returned home, he found that his hut was gone. In its place stood a fine cottage. Behind the cottage was a yard with cows and horses and chickens. And there was a vegetable garden full of cabbages and onions and potatoes.

The man and his wife were very happy. Time passed, and the woman said to her husband, 'Although we have plenty now, what good is it all unless we are important people? Go back to the tree and tell it to make you village elder.'

The man took up his axe and went into the forest. He stood before the magic tree and pretended he would strike it.

'What do you want?' asked the tree.

'My wife and I wish to be important people,' he said. 'Make me village elder.'

'It is already done,' said the tree.

And when the man returned home, he found that he was now a village elder. He and his wife were very happy. But not long afterwards, a band of soldiers came to their house and demanded to be given a place to stay and food to eat. They ordered the man about roughly and even struck him.

'What good is it to be village elder if soldiers can beat me?' said the man.

'But if we were nobles,' said his wife, 'people would have to treat us with respect. Go back to the tree and tell it to make you a count and me a countess.'

The man went back to the forest and stood before the magic tree. He raised his axe as if to strike.

'What do you want?' asked the tree.

'My wife and I wish to be nobles. Make us count and countess.'

'It is already done,' said the tree.

And when the man reached home, he discovered that he and his wife had been made count and countess. They lived happily for a time, but it was not very long before the woman said to her husband, 'To be nobles is not enough. However, if you were a colonel, we would be the envy of the other nobles.'

So the man went back to the forest again to ask the magic tree to grant their wish.

'What is it you want?' asked the tree.

'I want to be a colonel,' said the man.

'It is already done,' said the tree.

And when the man went home, he learned that he had been made a colonel in the Czar's army.

They were very happy, for all the other nobles envied them, but after a time, the man complained, 'Precious little good it does to be a colonel, if the general can command me to do anything he wants.'

'Then go back to the tree and tell it to make you a general,' said the woman.

The man returned once more to the magic tree.

'What do you want this time?' asked the tree.

'I want to be a general,' said the man.

'It is already done,' said the tree.

And when the man returned home, he found he had been promoted to general. But it was not long before he said, 'Being a general is no good at all, for the Czar can command me to do whatever he wishes.'

'Then go to the tree,' said his wife, 'and tell it to make you Czar.'

So the man went back to the tree again.

'What do you want now?' asked the tree.

'To be Czar,' said the man.

'It is already done,' said the tree.

And when he returned home from the forest, the news had already arrived that the old Czar was dead and that the man had been chosen as Czar and his wife as Czarina.

They moved into the palace and began to rule. And they were happy now because everyone had to obey their commands. But soon the man said, 'Ruling a country is a lot of hard work.'

'Being Czar and Czarina means very little,' said the woman, 'for at any moment, God can send death to us. Go to that tree and tell it to make us equal to God.'

The man set out for the forest, carrying his axe. He stood before the tree and raised the axe as if to strike.

'What more do you want?' demanded the tree.

The wind blew so fiercely around him that the man could hardly hear his own words. 'Make us equal to God,' he said.

But the tree shook its branches furiously and said, 'That can never be. As for you and your wife, by wanting too much you have lost all. Go now and come to me never again.'

The man returned home and found their riches gone and their titles no more and his wife no longer sitting in the palace but in their simple hut, as before. And there they lived to the end of their days.

The Monkeys' Treasure

Laos

Once there was a poor old man who lived at the edge of a jungle forest. All he had in the world was a melon patch, which he tended very carefully. Some of the fruit he ate himself, and some he sold to make a living, but there were still many melons left on the vines.

So he did not mind when the monkeys of the forest came into his garden and helped themselves to the sweet melons.

'What kind of man is this,' said the monkeys, 'who willingly shares such luscious fruit with us and does not chase us away, as the other farmers do? Here is an unusual man indeed!'

One day, the old man became very ill, so ill that he lay near death. When the monkeys came into the garden, they found him lying under a tree near the melon patch.

'The poor old man is dead,' they whispered. 'Since he kindly shared his melons with us, let us lay him to

rest in the finest place we can find.'

The monkeys lifted the old man onto their shoulders and carried him into the forest. Soon they came to a fork in the path. One of the monkeys said, 'Let us take him to the cave of silver.'

Another said, 'No, the cave of gold would be better.'

The others agreed. They followed a path deep into the forest to a cave, where they laid the old man to rest among piles of gleaming gold. Then the monkeys returned to the forest, leaving the old man all alone in the cave.

After a while, the old man felt well enough to stand up. He was astonished to find himself surrounded by more gold than he had ever imagined. He gathered up as much as he could carry. Then he made his way back to his home.

As he came up the path, his neighbour stared at the gold in surprise.

'How did you, who are only a gardener, come by such riches?' asked the neighbour. Willingly, the old man told him what had happened.

'If you did it so easily, I can surely trick those foolish monkeys myself,' thought the neighbour. And from that day on, instead of chasing away the monkeys when they came to eat the vegetables in his garden, he welcomed them and allowed them to eat their fill.

One day, the neighbour lay down in his garden and

pretended to be dead. When the monkeys came to the garden, they saw him there and carried him into the forest to find a place to lay him to rest. When they came to the fork in the path, the monkeys began to talk about which way they should take.

The man was thinking of how much gold he would carry away, and how he might even make a bamboo basket to drag along behind him so he could carry off even more gold, when one of the monkeys said, 'Let us take him to the cave of silver.'

'No! Take me to the cave of gold!' cried the man, forgetting that he was supposed to be dead. His shouts startled the monkeys so much that they dropped him at once and fled into the trees, leaving the greedy man without a single lump of gold, but with quite a lump on the head.

The Sunshine Tree

Sweden

Once there was an old woman who lived by herself in a little cottage at the edge of a forest. Her cottage was always swept clean, the floor strewn with fresh and fragrant rushes, and her door was always open to friend and stranger alike. Even when the day was dark and gloomy, inside the cottage it was always bright and sunny, for the light that shone in the window did not come from the sun, but from a wonderful pear tree that bore radiant white blossoms and shimmering golden fruit all year long. These white blossoms and golden fruit shone so brightly that it seemed as though the light of the sun itself blazed forth from the tree. And that is why everyone called it the Sunshine Tree.

From far away, people came to see the wonderful tree, and to every visitor the woman gave a silver seed from its fruit. When these seeds were planted in good soil and watered with care, they would grow into wondrous trees full of light, just like the Sunshine Tree they came from.

All those who came to visit the old woman accepted her gift with joy. But not all of them treated the seeds properly. Sometimes they planted them in poor soil, and sometimes they forgot to water them, so the plants never came up, or else they withered and died. Those who took care of their gifts were rewarded by seeing the little plants grow into sturdy trees heavy with blossoms and fruit that filled their homes with clear light. But none of these trees was quite as big or had quite such delicate blossoms or shimmering fruit as the old woman's Sunshine Tree.

A wealthy man who lived on the other side of the forest heard of the wondrous pear tree, and he sent his servant to buy it from the old woman. But of course the woman would not sell the tree, for who would sell the thing that filled one's heart and one's home with light all year round, even when it rained? No, she sent the servant back to his master with the message that she did not wish to sell her precious tree. But, out of kindness, she also sent the man a seed so that he could grow a sunshine tree of his own.

When the rich man heard her answer, he was furious, and he threw away the little seed with an unkind word. The next day, he himself went to see the old woman, to make her sell him the Sunshine Tree. 'I will give you a gold ducat for that tree!' he said.

Again, the old woman said no.

'Very well, ten ducats!' he shouted.

But her answer was the same. She would not sell her pear tree at any price.

The man went home without the tree, and in a very nasty mood. He sat in the dimmest corner of his gloomy mansion and sulked for a long time, until at last his mouth curled into an evil smile. 'I know how I can get the Sunshine Tree for myself,' he said. 'The old woman won't sell it, that's clear, but if I buy the land that the Sunshine Tree grows on, I can do with it what I like!'

Right away, the man sent his servant to town to buy the property that the old woman's house stood on — and her Sunshine Tree too. Soon the servant returned with the deed of ownership in hand.

The man could not even wait till morning. That night, he went to the old woman's cottage. As he came closer, he was amazed to see that the Sunshine Tree brightened even the night with its glow.

'I own this property now,' he announced, after waking the woman out of a sound sleep. 'And I'm having this tree removed in the morning. It will make a fine addition to *my* garden. I shall place it where it will send its rays right into the great hall of my mansion, which is always a little gloomy.'

'Please do not take the tree away from the soil in which it has grown,' said the old woman. 'For so many years it has brightened my home and my life. Please do not take it away.'

'This land belongs to me now, and everything that grows in the soil is mine,' he insisted. 'I will do what I please with it.'

'The tree may die if you dig it up,' she said.

But the man refused to listen, and the next morning, his servants and gardeners came to dig up the Sunshine Tree and carry it by cart to the mansion garden. But before they took the tree away, the old woman begged to have a tiny silver seed, and they saw no harm in letting her take one. She planted it in the place where the Sunshine Tree had grown.

Outside the great hall of the mansion, the gardeners dug a hole, and there they planted the pear tree. They propped it up with silver sticks and they watered it with golden watering cans. But its branches drooped, and its light seemed less than before. The very next day, every blossom dropped from the tree. The day after that, all the fruit withered and fell off. On the following day, all the leaves fluttered to the ground. The tree that once had been so strong and bright was now bare and lifeless.

But in the place where the Sunshine Tree had grown, the seed that the old woman planted had sprouted, and the young pear tree grew quickly. Soon it was as tall as the old tree had been, and its delicate blossoms and golden fruit shone just as brightly. It was almost as if the spirit of the Sunshine Tree had come back again with just as much brilliance and light. The old woman was very happy.

Soon the wealthy man heard the news that the old woman had a new Sunshine Tree. He lost no time in coming to claim it for himself.

'It must be the soil,' he said. 'There must be something in this soil here that can be found nowhere else. I shall build a new mansion right here, beside the Sunshine Tree. That means you'll have to leave.'

He ordered the old woman to take all her belongings and move out of her cottage at once. The little cottage was torn down, and masons and carpenters began to build a new mansion on the spot.

The old woman begged to be allowed to take a single seed from her beloved tree, but the man said, 'I can't allow that. This tree is all mine, you see, and it would not be so rare and valuable if everyone had one like it. Be off.'

But before she left, she went to her tree to say good-bye. To those who watched, it seemed that the pear tree bent down its boughs and branches around the old woman as if to comfort her, and it seemed as though, in the forest close by, the pine trees swayed and whispered among themselves. But then the tree stood up again, as still as before. They shook their heads and told themselves that they must have been mistaken, and that it was only the wind that whispered.

The old woman's neighbours gave her a piece of

ground where she could see the forest and the pear tree, and they built her another cottage, which was finished the same day as the new mansion.

The wealthy man held a great party to celebrate. In fancy, gilt carriages his guests arrived and gathered in the great hall to see the marvellous pear tree that was rumoured to shine with the splendour of the sun.

'Wonderful! Enchanting! Superb!' they cried, and they clapped their hands and congratulated the owner of such a rare thing. The man was very proud of himself, for never had people envied him so.

All of a sudden a young girl pointed at the tree and said, 'Look! It even moves.'

It was true. The tree began to spread its branches until they looked like great shining wings. It moved them up and down, as if the pear tree were trying to pull itself out of the earth. Suddenly its roots came free of the soil and the tree flew up, over the heads of the astonished guests. It flew over the fields and hedges until it came to the old woman's cottage. It set its roots down deep into the ground and soon it looked as though it had always grown right there.

With tears of joy in her eyes, the old woman rushed out to greet the Sunshine Tree. She kissed its branches and leaves, so happy was she to have her beloved tree near her once more.

Inside the mansion, the light had faded. The Sunshine Tree was gone, but the hall grew darker still.

The guests huddled together in fear, for quite soon it was as dark as night. The trees of the forest had crept up close to the mansion and now surrounded it, blocking all light from the windows so that inside it seemed as if night had fallen. The bewildered guests fled from the place, shrieking in terror. And with them, most terrified of all, ran the owner of the mansion, who never came back to torment the old woman and her pear tree again.